Look and Find®

ILLUMINATION PRESENTS

THE SECRET LIFE OF PETS 2

Adapted by Erin Rose Wage
Illustrated by Art Mawhinney

we make books come alive®
pi kids® Phoenix International Publications, Inc.
Chicago • London • New York • Hamburg • Mexico City • Paris • Sydney

It's another lovely day for besties Max and Duke, their owner Katie, and her new husband Chuck. Katie is going to have a baby! Max and Duke check out the kids playing in Central Park. Duke loves the youngsters! But Max feels a little nervous.
SNACKS
NY
NY

Take a walk through the park and spot these rowdy rascals:

Once baby Liam is born, Duke is thrilled! It takes Max a little while, but eventually he grows to love Liam *so much* that he becomes anxious. He wants to make sure Liam is safe from all the scary things they might encounter in the big city...like chewed-up gum, scooters, and pigeons!

Lace up your walking shoes and help Max “protect” Liam from these “perils”:

- chewed-up gum
- big fire truck
- hissing sewer grate steam
- unpredictable scooter
- loud car horn
- superfast in-line skater
- orange construction cone
- spraying sprinkler

Max's worrying has made him itchy. Now he scratches. And *scratches*. And SCRATCHES! Katie takes him for a walk—one of Max's favorite things—but what's this? A veterinarian's office?! Max has been tricked! And there isn't even anything wrong with him!

As Max gets in a quick scratch, check the waiting room for these antsy animals:

gift-giving cat

perturbed parrot

good dog

fire-starting kitties

troubled turtle

hamster who's going nowhere

wide-eyed beagle

feisty ferret

The vet puts a cone on Max to stop him from scratching. Then Katie decides that the best medicine for Max is rest and relaxation on Chuck's family farm. So Max brings his favorite toy Busy Bee to Gidget for safekeeping, and hits the road! The country is so different from the city. The sounds and smells—and turkeys—are alarming!

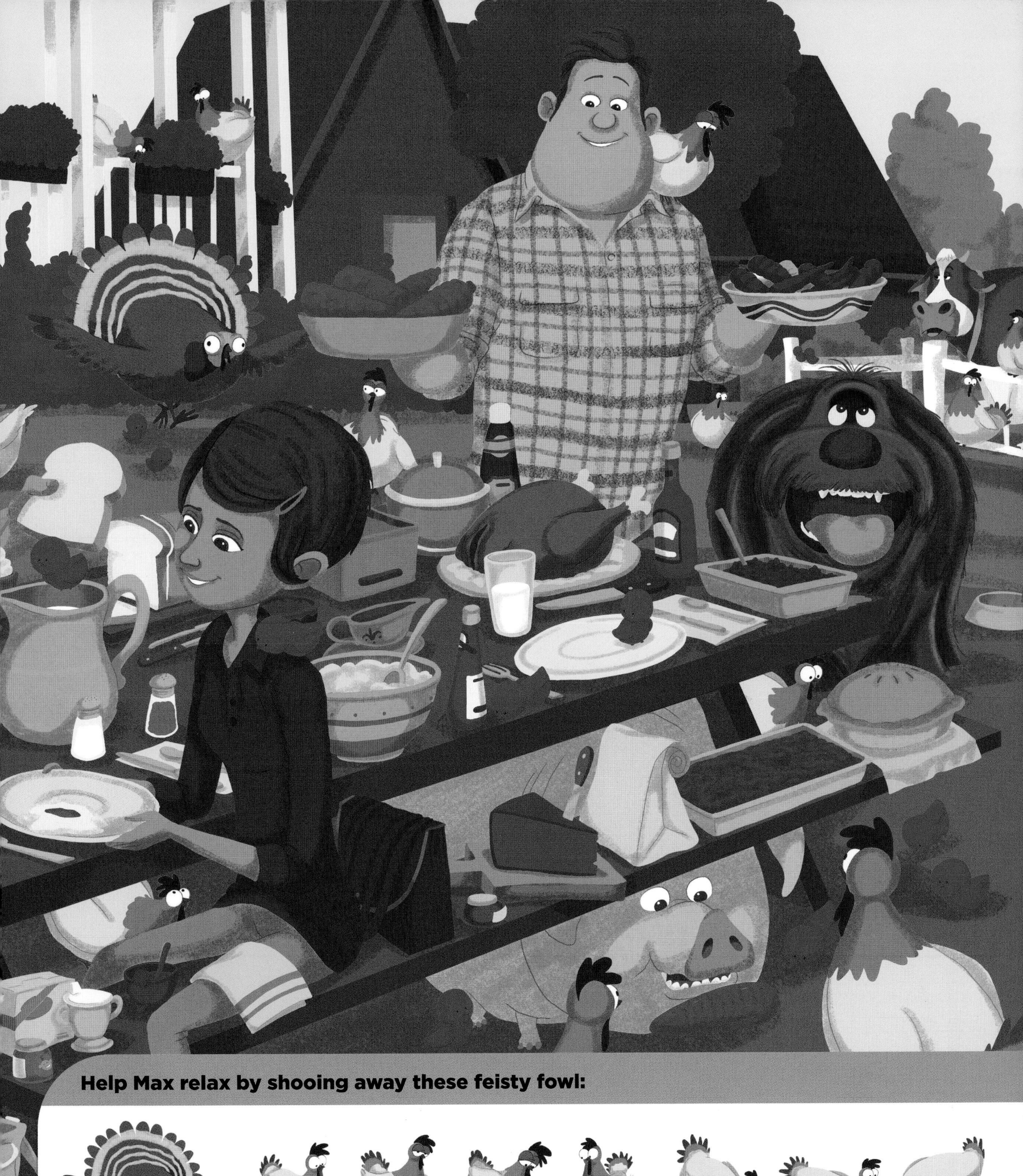

Help Max relax by shooing away these feisty fowl:

Back in the city, Snowball has been playing superhero. His first case is to help his new friend Daisy rescue a tiger cub named Hu from a circus. But Hu is guarded by wolves...and trouble ensues for the little white bunny as he sprints through the circus's carnival. Luckily Daisy is on her way to save the day!

In the meantime, help Snowball blend into these carnival surroundings:

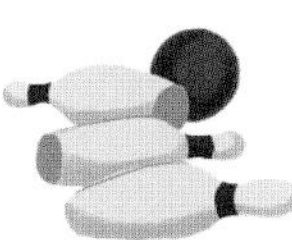
bowling game

ring toss game

duck-pond ducks

bunny prize

water cannon

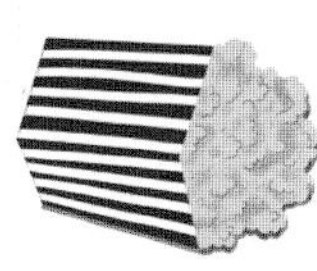
broken popcorn sign

cotton candy sign

bunch of balloons

Daisy, Snowball, and Hu escape the circus and head over to Pops' apartment, which is now home to a puppy school. Snowball asks Pops for help watching the tiger cub. After all, Pops is already caring for a ton of puppies. What's one more little tiger?

Roll over with these cute little critters:

Uh-oh. Busy Bee has fallen into an apartment FILLED with cats! Gidget needs to use her canine cunning to rescue Max's favorite toy before he returns from the farm. Chloe teaches Gidget how to behave like a cat and helps her create a feline disguise. Norman is ready in the air duct with a laser pointer in case things get...catty.

As Gidget does her best catwalk through the apartment, help her avoid these felines:

Out on the farm, Max has been spending a lot of time with Rooster, a super-cool herding dog with a relaxed attitude. Rooster teaches Max not to worry so much. He even frees Max from his cone! Max starts to feel better and decides to try his paw at herding.

Before Max goes home to his beloved Busy Bee, help him herd these wayward sheep:

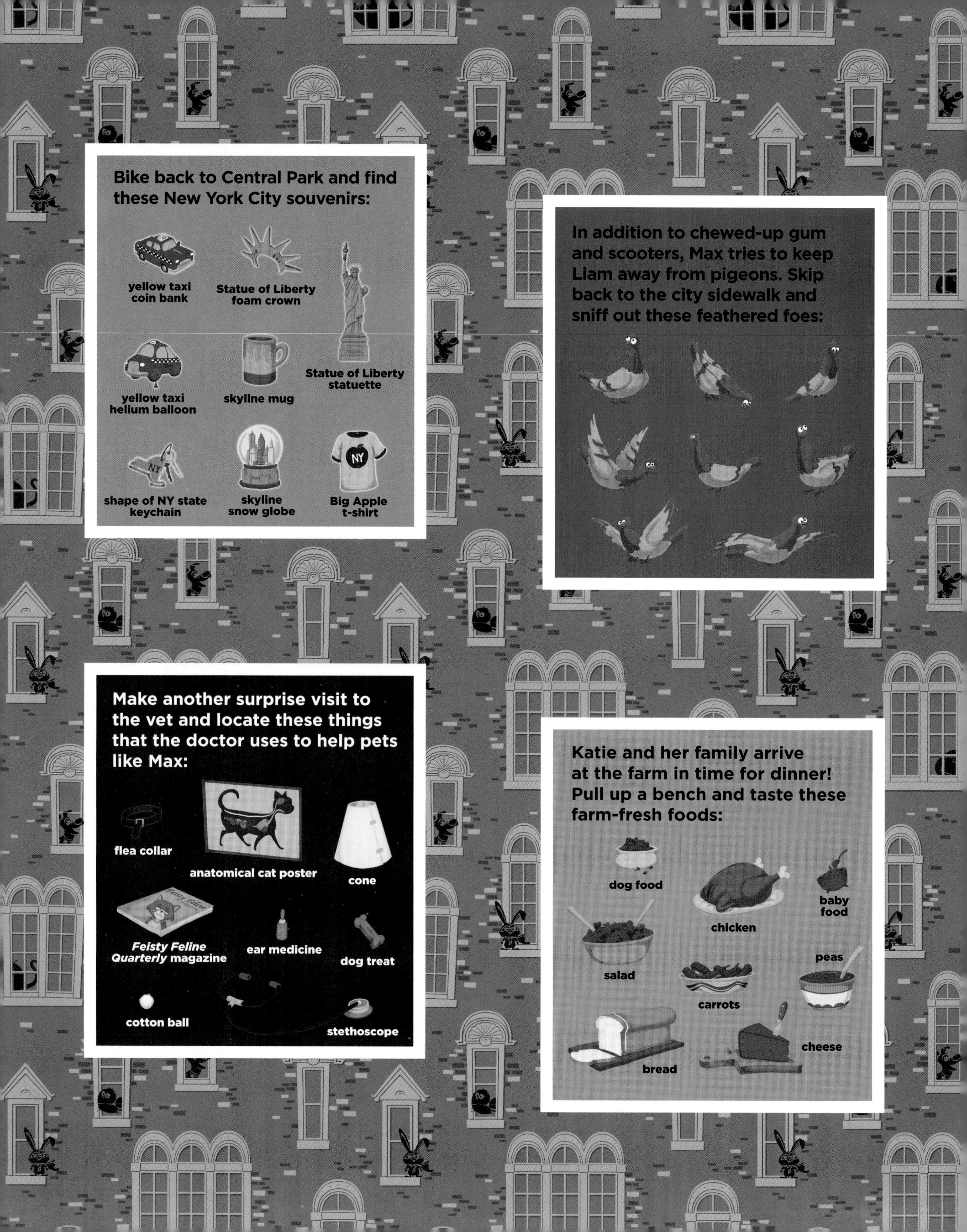
Bike back to Central Park and find these New York City souvenirs:
yellow taxi coin bank
Statue of Liberty foam crown
Statue of Liberty statuette
yellow taxi helium balloon
skyline mug
shape of NY state keychain
skyline snow globe
Big Apple t-shirt
In addition to chewed-up gum and scooters, Max tries to keep Liam away from pigeons. Skip back to the city sidewalk and sniff out these feathered foes:
Make another surprise visit to the vet and locate these things that the doctor uses to help pets like Max:
flea collar
anatomical cat poster
cone
Feisty Feline Quarterly magazine
ear medicine
dog treat
cotton ball
stethoscope
Katie and her family arrive at the farm in time for dinner! Pull up a bench and taste these farm-fresh foods:
dog food
chicken
baby food
salad
peas
carrots
bread
cheese

Ding! Ding! Ding! Circle back to the circus carnival and collect
20
tickets.
If there's one thing puppies love, it's socks...and not a pair of them, just one. Prance back to the puppy school at Pops' and find these stolen single socks:
Sneak back into the cat apartment and find these things the cats have put their special mark on:
bitten book cover
pounced picture frame
nudged lampshade
pawed porcelain cat figurine
cut curtains
toppled clock
ripped rug
clawed couch
Max is feeling so much better! Make your way baaaack to the sheep herd and find these things that used to make Max worry:
fox
small bird
chicken
big turkey
pig
frog
cricket
squirrel eating corn